SESAME STREET

THE THREE LITTLE
GROUCHES

Hey! Learn these four great words: grouch, grouches, grouchy, grouchiest!

Adapted from the original story by Jodie Shepherd

LEVEL **1** READER

READING LEVEL

Published by Dalmatian Press, LLC. All rights reserved.
Printed in Luogang, Guangdong, China.

Once upon a time,
there were three little grouches.
The first was Oscar the Grouch.
He was the grouchiest of all.

Oscar made his can smelly with
one rotten banana and yucky fish.
"Heh-heh!" he said.
"What a grouchy smell!"

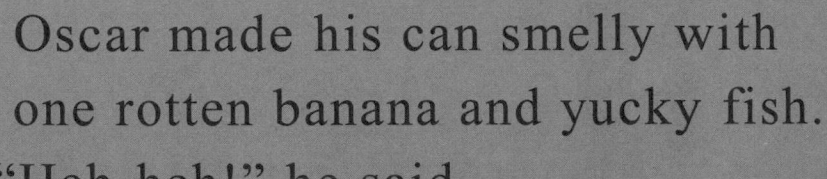

The second was Zoe the Grouch.
She made her can smelly with
two rotten bananas and old socks.
"Yeah!" said Zoe.
"What a grouchy smell."

The third was Elmo the Grouch.
He made his can smelly with
three rotten bananas and stinky cheese.
"Hee-hee!" said Elmo.
"What a grouchy smell!"

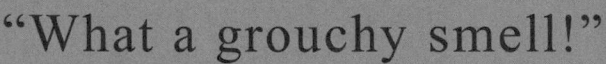

The three little trash cans
made one big smell.

"I smell something rotten!"
said Super Grover.

He looked down
at the three trash cans.
"Rotten bananas! Yucky fish!
Old socks! Stinky cheese!
That is one super-stinky mess!"

"Well, *who* asked *you*?"
called Oscar.

Those three little grouches were *very*, *very* grouchy! They were only happy when the trash truck came by.

One day, an old shoe fell out of the trash truck.

"Yes!" said Oscar. "Time for a game of Kick the Old Shoe!"

Just then, along came
Big Bad Snuffleupagus.
(Well, okay. He wasn't bad,
but he was very BIG!)

Snuffleupagus walked up to
the can of the first little
grouch with the rotten banana
and yucky fish.

Snuffleupagus said nicely,
"Little grouch, little grouch,
please clean this mess."

"This mess is too big to clean!"
said Oscar.

"Then I'll huff and I'll puff and I'll blow it away," said Snuffleupagus.

And he did. He huffed and puffed and blew the rotten banana and yucky fish all the way to the trash truck.

Then Snuffleupagus came to the can of the second little grouch with the rotten bananas and old socks.

"Little grouch, little grouch, please clean this mess," he said nicely.

"This mess is too big to clean," said grouch number two.

"Then I'll huff and I'll puff and I'll blow it away," said Big Bad Snuffleupagus.

And he did. He huffed and puffed and blew the rotten bananas and old socks all the way to the trash truck.

Then Snuffleupagus came to the can of the third little grouch with the rotten bananas and stinky cheese.

"Little grouch, little grouch, please clean this mess," he said nicely.

"This mess is too big to clean," said grouch number three.

"Then I'll huff and I'll puff and I'll blow it away," said Big Bad Snuffleupagus.

And he did. He huffed and puffed and blew the rotten bananas and stinky cheese all the way to the trash truck.

And the trash truck drove away.

"Hmmmm. . ." said Zoe. "Not bad. I think I like being nice and neat."

"Elmo, too!" said Elmo. "Elmo liked being grouchy, but now Elmo loves being clean and happy!"

"It sounded like you needed some help to clean up those bananas and fish and socks and cheese," said Snuffleupagus.

"Oh, yes!" said Zoe.
"The street smells better, too!"

Elmo gave Snuffleupagus a hug. "Thank you for the huffs and puffs!" Elmo said.

"Thank you?" Oscar grumbled.
"What kind of grouches *are* you?
Get lost—and have a rotten day!"

"Come on," said Zoe. "Let's go
get some bananas that are
not rotten!"

"Elmo loves bananas!" said Elmo.
"And Elmo loves you, too,
Oscar, even though you are
still grouchy!"

"Now, that's just yucky!"
said Oscar.